# WITHIN
# TREMBLING
# CAVERNS

Never forget to
feed the dragon...

G. Jeffrey

# Within Trembling Caverns

## DARK FOLKLORE

### Georgina Jeffery

Coblyn Press

First published by Coblyn Press 2022

Cover designed by GetCovers

First edition

ISBN: 978-1-8381498-5-7

georginajeffery.com

'Tell us the one about the dragon, Babcia.'

I chuckled deep into my scarf as my grandchildren gathered around me. Agata, the youngest, was only four years old. She clutched at my knee, blinking owlishly with her sweet brown eyes. She was flanked by her cousins, Emil, Filip, and Henryk (sturdy boys, triplets aged eight from my daughter Ivanka) and her brother Pawel, who would turn thirteen next month.

They shuffled with their bookbags and lunchboxes, silently matching my gaze with their own expectant stares.

I straightened my back, placed my hands on my knees and addressed them like a court from my armchair. 'Who told you there was a dragon?'

They threw perplexed glances between them. I could hear them thinking: *this isn't how Babcia usually starts a story.*

Pawel spoke up for them. 'You did, Babcia. Last

1

time we were here. You said you'd feed us to the dragon if we didn't eat all our dinner.'

'It lives in a cave,' Henryk added excitedly.

'Has big teeth,' said Emil.

'And gobbles up children!' exclaimed Filip.

'*Roar*,' whispered Agata.

I smiled, nodding to each of their outbursts. 'So I did, so I did. How foolish of me! But surely such stories aren't for children.'

'*Please*, Babcia!' they chorused.

Their voices were a balm for all the sore spots in my soul. I carried the mantle of *Babcia* with such great pride for these darlings. Once, I might have scoffed at the thought that I would enjoy being called 'Grandmother' so often, and so fervently. But how could anyone refuse the adoration from these shining, innocent faces?

The children inched closer on their knees with cheeky, pleading smiles. I gave a theatrical sigh and relented – the long-foregone conclusion to this artificial conflict.

'Oh, all right. This is the story of the Wawel Dragon,' I began. 'You've heard of it, yes? The dragon that terrorised our very city in days of old. Back then, Kraków was not so large as it is today.'

I swept a hand to the window – somewhat pointlessly, because it only showed my unkempt, weed-ridden garden. My house stood on the outermost suburbs of the old capital city, a short walk from the countryside and the Vistula River.

Nevertheless, I ploughed on with aplomb: 'It began as a small town on Wawel Hill, where the Royal Castle now stands. The town was surrounded by many farmers rearing cattle, and it would have been a prosperous time. If it weren't for the dragon.'

Pawel jittered with the urge to interrupt. 'Where did it live?' he burst in.

'Sit down, lad, I'm getting to that,' I said. 'In the lands beneath the hill, looking over the farmers' fields, there was a cave. This is where the dragon dwelled . . . and ruled. The whole town was beholden to its dreadful appetite. *"Feed me!"* the dragon demanded every day, *"else I'll gobble up all your children!"*

I was rather proud of the monstrous voice I'd chosen for the dragon. Agata let out a little gasp, but it didn't stop her shuffling forward just as eagerly as her older cousins.

'So what did the people in the town do?' Filip asked anxiously.

I folded my hands in my lap, darkening my expression to a sombre frown. 'They had no choice, of course. Once every month, they selected a young virgin to feed to the dragon. Off to the cave they went, with the weight of the town on their shoulders, never to be seen again.'

Pawel's eyes lit up with mischief. 'What's a vir–'

'It was a terrible time,' I intervened quickly. 'The townsfolk were awash with grief. Until one day, they'd had enough. Or more rightly, a cobbler had had enough.'

'What's a cob–'

'They make *shoes*,' Emil butted in proudly.

I patted him on the shoulder. 'That's right,' I agreed. 'A lowly shoemaker. And he had a fine plan to beat the dragon.'

'What did he do?' asked Henryk.

I mimed the action of opening and stuffing a bag with my hands. 'He took the skin of a calf and crammed it full of sulphur and hay, and tinder cloth. He set this on fire and sewed it up, while the sulphur continued to smoulder inside. Then he crept up to the dragon's cave and laid the thing down at the entrance. He spilled some pig's blood around it to mask the smell. Then off he went to hide. And not a moment too soon. For out came the dragon.' I stretched my neck forward like a turtle from my scarf and the children cowered away.

'It sniffed the air,' I said, flaring my nostrils. 'Its tongue salivated.' I snapped my jaws together. 'It reached down to the little calf skin . . . *and gobbled it up!*'

The children shrieked as I launched off my chair. I caught Agata about her middle and soon had her in fits of giggles as I tickled her. The children broke into laughter and gathered around me again.

'What did the sulphur do to the dragon?' Pawel said excitedly. 'Did it burn it from the inside out?'

I lowered myself back into my chair. 'Of a sort,' I said thoughtfully. 'The sulphur smouldered in the dragon's throat. So painful, it was! So hot and dry. And it made the dragon so very thirsty. So off it went to the nearest river and stuck its head full in.'

'*Splash*,' Agata said quietly, eliciting more giggles.

'It drank and it drank,' I continued, 'and it drank and drank and drank until finally . . . its stomach swelled to bursting and the dragon couldn't possibly drink any more – and yet, it did! As the last drops slid down its gullet, the dragon's stomach *burst*. Split wide open, it did, spilling water across the ground. And that was how the dragon died. All thanks to the cobbler's brilliant plan.'

'Then what?' asked Pawel.

'The town lived happily ever after,' I replied.

'No, no,' he said. 'To the dragon.'

I raised an eyebrow. 'It was dead, child.'

He bounced impatiently on his knees. In his hands he knotted and unknotted his woolly scarf, a stripy yellow-green treasure of my own making. 'But what did they do with the *body?*' he insisted.

I masked a little sigh, though it fast became a smile. That was Pawel all over. And I knew there was only one thing that would satisfy him. I beckoned him closer.

'Well now. The dragon had burst open, remember? Its bits were splattered all across the riverbank. It lay in great sopping piles. A piece of intestine here, an eyeball there . . . The sack of its stomach spilled all its putrid acids across the ground, including a half-digested cow.' I put a hand to my forehead. 'And the *stench*, oh! The awful smells that wafted towards the town–'

'*Babcia!*' My daughter Ivanka appeared in the doorway. Her mouth was set in a thin, disapproving line, like it was disappearing in on itself. 'Must you say such things?'

'It's only a story,' I said lightly, settling back into my cushions.

Ivanka's mouth near twisted itself off her face. She glared at my grandkids. 'Up, children, come on. We'll be late.'

Reluctantly, Pawel and the others rose from the floor and pecked me a kiss on the cheek.

Pawel snatched a whisper into my ear. 'Do you think its bones could still be there?'

'Almost certainly,' I said, giving him a hug.

Ivanka tapped her foot while the children filed past her. When they'd all been counted and were outside in the hall to get their shoes on, she crossed the room to speak to me.

'You can't watch them for even half an hour without resorting to monstrous stories?' she accused.

'They enjoy my fairy tales,' I said airily. 'A grandmother is supposed to weave such yarns.'

'With *intestines?*'

'It would be a struggle, but yes I imagine you could weave with–'

'*Mother.*' Ivanka pinched the bridge of her nose. 'Could you take this seriously, please? Is now really the right time for grotesque tales?'

I reached for her other hand, enclosed it in both my palms. 'Yes,' I said gently. 'Now is the exact time these sorts of stories are needed most.'

Ivanka's face relaxed a little. She let me stroke her hand for a moment longer. Then whipped it away. 'Can you watch the triplets for me tomorrow evening? Pawel needs someone to attend his school meeting. With the counsellor.'

'His mother can't do it?' I asked, though it wasn't really a question.

'She's still . . . very ill,' Ivanka replied.

'I see.' This was code. Pawel and Agata's mother was still lost at the bottom of a bottle somewhere.

The kids shuffled in the hallway. Ivanka strode

to the door, calling a roll call of coats and hats and schoolbags like a sergeant running a kit check. Satisfied her platoon was fully equipped, she tipped me a tight smile and marched her squad to the door.

'Have a good day at school, lovelies,' I called after them. 'And watch out for dragons.'

The heavy clunk of the lock echoed on the tiles. The house gained a layer of sudden chill, having lost the warmth of little smiling faces.

I remained in my armchair a while, sucking a lemon sweet from the tin in my skirt pocket.

On the wall, the ticking of my pendulum clock provided some company next to my husband's portrait: a much younger man in that photo, but the fierce, intelligent stare had been a mark of his personality to the end. In the portrait he held a brass pocket watch, his most treasured thing. What a shame, everyone always said, that we don't even have that to remember him by.

Though I doubted my children wanted to remember him much at all.

Ivanka blamed me, I think, for the broken pieces of the family she was now picking up. Because surely it was a matter of upbringing, for

Jozef to walk out on his children, just like his own father did to him.

At least we knew where Jozef was. My foolish son was safe, drinking mojitos on a beach in the Caribbean somewhere with his new lady friend. Agata was too young to understand. But Pawel had taken to skipping school, and by many accounts was turning into a wild child when he wasn't in Ivanka's care.

*Or mine,* I thought smugly. My stories gave Pawel something to focus on.

My clock chimed the hour – clunkily, in need of some mechanical repair. The tinny noise pulled me from reverie.

'Come on, you old maid,' I said to myself. 'Ivanka will have you in a home for invalids if you sit still all day.'

I rose from my armchair and shambled into the kitchen, ignoring the twinge of arthritis in my ankles. Other bits of me lined up to share their grievances: new atrophies and old injuries stored in my bones. Each was turned away. There were jobs to be done.

I swept a stack of magazines out of the way and opened my fridge. My nose wrinkled at the smell of sour milk, and I made a note to deal with that later. But for now, a more pressing errand held my attention. I plucked a large carrier bag from the nearest pile and filled it with two shrink-wrapped roast chickens and a string of fresh sausages.

In the hallway I exchanged my slippers for orthopaedic shoes. By the door, a small rubber mallet sat on a little shelf next to my keys. I tucked it into the bag. Shrugged on my overcoat, pulled the scarf up over my head to keep the wind off, and opened my front door. Crisp autumn air filled my lungs.

The breeze carried the fresh sedimentary smells of the Vistula. I walked against it in the direction of the riverbank. Houses were thin out on the trailing outskirts of the city – a sprawl of villages and fields following the path of the river. I cut across a patch of scrubby woodland, heading north, leaving the Vistula behind me.

The path soon led down a steep slope. If you were foolish enough to diverge from it (which I did) you could stumble your way over nettles and along a somewhat sheer edge as the rest of the forest floor fell away from you. Eventually this precipice levelled out again, and the only way was down. From here the trick was to go from tree to tree. I made the slowest of progress as I carefully felt around with every footstep for fear of shifting soil or hidden tree roots.

At the bottom, I entered a natural gulley where a greater number of stones poked through the earth. I followed this rocky trail until, finally, I reached a clearing of sorts . . . and the entrance to a cave.

A padded bed of leaves cushioned my footsteps as I approached. The cave was a wide, dark gash in the rock, mostly hidden under an overhanging stone. I would need to crawl if I'd wanted to go inside it. Happily, I didn't.

I set down my bulging carrier bag and collapsed onto a smooth rock nearby. Stretching out my legs, I tipped my head back and let the cool woody air carry away some of my exhaustion.

After a while, I clapped my hands at the cave entrance.

'Come on, you old Smok,' I called into it. 'I haven't got all day.'

Something wheezed in the darkness. By degrees, a rasping and crunching sound emerged from deep within the cave. The shrill grinding of stone – the sound of pebbles against a cheese-grater – put my teeth on edge.

'Careful of them stalactites,' I said. 'Or stalag-mites. I can never remember which. My neigh-bour Ruta's always going on about it. Important geological whatsits, anyway.'

'Oh, shut up, you old witch,' rasped a shadow in the darkness.

'Manners,' I said, 'or you'll lose your dinner.'

Accompanied by another round of wheezy grumbling, the shadow hauled itself towards the light.

The snout appeared first. Covered in pale scales, it poked out of the crack that was only just wide enough for it to nose through.

Two massive, gnarled claws came next: they dug into the ground outside the cave. Tendons pulled taut under frail, scaly skin as exertion poured into the muscles surrounding them. With more grinding and crunching, the dragon dragged itself forward along the ground, chipping away at valuable cave formations while its horned head pushed up and out into the fresh morning air.

Milky blue eyes blinked in the direction of the sun. Nostril slits flared and the wide, flat lizard head swung in my direction. Its forked tongue flicked out to taste the world.

'*Food,*' the dragon hissed between rows of pock-marked teeth. Once they would have been sharp as daggers, shining like ivory. Now they were stained yellow, blunted, and plenty missing from the dragon's frilly pink gums.

I rustled around in my carrier bag, unwrapping a chicken. 'Soon I'll have to make these into soup for you,' I remarked.

'I do not eat soup.'

'You may have to, old lad.' I now pulled out the rubber mallet. Crude, I know, but effective. Laying the first chicken on the rock beside me, I set about smashing it to pieces.

'Quick, quick,' said the dragon, writhing its head to and fro.

I set aside my mallet. 'Open up.'

Jaws gaped wide. I tossed a fistful of chicken in. The dragon pitched its chin toward the sky, gulping raggedly, almost like a cat choking on a hairball. Slivers of meat fell out of the gaps in its teeth and slapped wetly onto the ground.

'More,' it demanded, opening its mouth to me again.

'You want to go slower,' I said, 'chew your food. Else one of these days you'll choke.'

The jaws snapped at me. 'I am no cow. I do not *chew*. I rip and tear the flesh. The bones dissolve in my many stomachs.'

'Still,' I said, smacking the mallet into the chicken's breastbone, 'would be a shame if that's the way you go. I have trouble with toffees from time to time, myself.'

I paused in thought before throwing another lump of carcass to the dragon. 'I've wondered how my children will find me, eventually. I hope it's all tucked up nicely in bed. But like as not it'll be in some mundanely embarrassing way. Just hope it's not on the toilet, is all I ask. I knew an old girl who passed away of a heart attack – God rest her soul – while doing her business in a public stall. I'd die all over again. But at least they say she didn't even feel it happen.'

The dragon tried to snap at the meat in my hand, but it was out of reach. I paid it no mind and continued my train of thought. 'Choking, now, that one scares me. Just as undignified, and all the time to think hard about how you should've chewed just that few seconds longer, or not been laughing while you swallowed – I have to tell Pawel off for that all the time. And all the while your lips turn blue and your body convulses–'

'*Woman.*' The great snout swung at me. 'Cease your prattling! Feed me!'

I dropped the mallet with an emphatic *clack* on the rock. 'I shan't feed you anything, if you speak to me like that.'

The claws curled. Smok raked its talons through the soil, putting me in mind of a bull about to charge. But I knew it wouldn't. I was safe from old Smok, so long as I still had a steady supply of chicken to come.

Still, the dragon gave a gurgling growl and bawled some threats at me. 'You *owe* me, woman! What of your debt? Would you like to hear your crimes screamed from the hillsides?'

I sighed, begrudgingly picking up another handful of meat. 'All bluster, you are,' I said, and tossed it in.

The dragon's jaws snapped again. It repeated the same disgusting guzzle.

Out came the tongue, quivering in what I'd come to consider an expression of cruel amusement. 'The woman knows her place. Look how your feeble desires have twisted. They have made a slave of you.'

I began slowly unwrapping the second chicken. 'I'm nobody's slave, old Smok,' I said in a good-natured way, though my tone held a warning. 'You might do well to consider me your carer, old boy. I don't see anyone else bringing you fat birds to munch on. What if I were to go away, hey? I'd like to see you catch a chicken on your own – ha!' I brought down the mallet with a satisfying *thunk*.

Smok, in its usual manner, wasn't at all perturbed. 'I have caught more wily meals in my time than chickens,' it hissed. Its nostrils huffed in excitement. 'Children make for entertaining prey. They are fast, but not strong, and the meat is tender and it is fun to hear them *squeal*–'

'Enough of that,' I said. 'No more talk of eating children.'

The dragon's head lolled to the side, mournfully. 'I miss such meals. With the snapping of bone and the running of juices. I would like to eat a child again–'

'*You shan't have any.*'

The mallet rattled out of my grasp. Smok's milky eyes narrowed at me.

'I will catch one if I like,' it sulked.

I blew out a composed breath. I should be used to Smok's silly mind games by now. 'What nonsense is this?' I said. 'You couldn't catch a child to save your life. Look at you. You can barely drag yourself out of your cave.'

'I do not need to,' Smok replied slyly. 'Children are so curious. They used to play here often. Sometimes I still hear them nearby.'

The dragon raised its head to the hillside as if sniffing out a memory. It continued speaking in a crooning voice, on the verge of being a rhyme. 'Come to my cave little ones, don't be scared. Come play in these depths little children, let me show you my lair. Such wonders, such treasures . . .'

I thumped my bag down on its nose. 'Enough! If you're going to talk like this, then you won't have any more to eat.'

I re-wrapped the chicken and began gathering up the rest of the meal. The dragon writhed at my feet.

'Do not take it away,' it growled. 'I am hungry. *I am hungry!*

'Serve you right,' I said, carefully folding the empty packets. I retrieved the mallet and rocked myself up onto my feet. 'Let this be a lesson. If you can't show some consideration, then you shan't get any in return. You can wait 'til next week for the rest of your chicken.'

'*She-witch*,' the dragon snarled, pawing at the ground. '*Foul whore.* I will devour you, and all your kin! I will crunch your bones and spit out your worthless withered soul. I will smear your entrails across the land.'

I shook my head and turned away from it. 'To think I pity you.'

Smok continued bawling as I withdrew from its lair. I scrambled up the steep bank – opposite to the direction I'd arrived, and certainly not an ideal path out. But at the top, a little way beyond the trees, there was an overgrown walking trail which connected this patch of woods to a park in my village. It was barely used. A great tangle of stinging plants deterred all but the most determined adventurers from exploring it.

Before reaching the trail, I checked the trees at the top of the slope. They bore a collection of rotting wooden signs. *Warning. Steep Drop. Keep Out. Danger Ahead.*

I would have to touch up the paint on them, I decided. A few were in need of replacing altogether.

I tramped on to the footpath and came out blinking, surprised, into bright sunlight overhead. A tremor of worry fluttered under my ribs. Someone – a kind soul, no doubt – had cut back the encroaching forest from the path. It was now a clear trail stretching into the distance. No more waist-high stinging nettles to wade through. And, as if purposely put there to compound my fear, I discovered fresh footprints in the mud.

I wondered how far the dragon's voice could carry.

'Enough of that,' I said under my breath. 'He's an old fool. All smoke without fire.'

Still, I lingered. My grandchildren played in the park by this trail. It was all very well when this was only a forgotten nook, near impassable for weeds. But if people walked by here often now . . .

Maybe old Smok's time was up?

The thought weighed heavy on my chest. I

didn't doubt Smok's taste for human flesh. It was certainly not a noble or morally decent creature worth saving. But I was in no position to pass judgement there.

Deep down, I knew that was why I fed the dragon.

What's the old proverb? Once you make your bed, this is how you must lie . . .

Looking back into the shadows of the trees, I glimpsed a few of my crumbling signs in the dim light. I considered whether I still had it in me to construct a fence of some kind. Smok was right about something: children were too curious for their own good, and a few limp warning signs probably wouldn't be enough.

I started down the path, grateful, at least in some small part, for the prospect of an easier journey home. My knees and ankles had already filed their complaints, and I was feeling extra brittle after the climb up the steep bank. The bag was still heavy in my hand, pulling on tired shoulders.

Perhaps in all this I let my guard down. Perhaps my walk slowed to shuffle at the wrong moment. Perhaps it was sheer carelessness that led my foot to catch on a raised tree root and topple me, in ludicrous slow motion, hands outstretched, spilling sausages as I plunged toward the ground.

I landed with a searing *crack* in my left ankle. It was quickly followed by a deep, intense pain in my shin muscles. It ran all the way up my leg to my hip, spurring nausea in my stomach. I spat soil from my mouth. *Call for help,* I thought dimly.

'Help,' I croaked ineffectually.

The contents of my bag lay scattered somewhere out of sight. My scarf had flown forward over my face so I could barely see. I lifted my head, placed my weight on my right arm – in doing so I must have twisted slightly, in just the wrong way, because it sent a spike of agony through my leg and I collapsed back into a pathetic heap.

'Please, anyone,' I mumbled into the dirt. I was terrified by the feebleness of my own voice. Had I always been such an old woman?

The wind blew down the path, fluttering my scarf up away from my eyes and permeating my many layers. I registered that the earth was damp, and the cold was creeping into my bones.

'Worse than choking,' I muttered. Then would

have slapped myself, if I could. *You are not going to die here, Truda, alone in the woods.*

With a long, low groan, I pulled myself up onto one hand and knee, carefully keeping my left side limp as a fish. I could drag myself, I thought. Inch by inch.

Muffled footsteps reached my ears. Pounding on the mossy earth, someone running. The footsteps landed at my side.

'Careful,' said a welcome, warm voice. 'Are you hurt, lady? Should I call someone?'

'Ivanka,' I burbled. 'Call my daughter.'

I shifted again, sparking another crackling tide of pain. The world swam in front of my eyes. I mumbled a string of numbers, listened with only half an ear as the man held a muted phone conversation, and then it was a blur of cold and waiting and cold, and suddenly people and pain, and being lifted and pain and jolting around under bright lights while many, many people talked over me, and Ivanka looking down at me with stiffness in her lips and hard edges to her eyes, until something was slipped into my mouth and I finally rested deeply, and silently.

*\* \* \**

'Tell us about the dragon again, Babcia.'

I passed a hand over my eyes. 'Not now, children. Perhaps another story.'

'Please,' whined Emil, with his two brothers providing dejected expressions of support over his shoulder.

'*Boys.*' Ivanka's warning echoed from the kitchen. 'Leave Babcia alone. She needs to rest.'

Agata gently poked the plastic boot that encased my left foot. 'Is it getting better?'

I forced a faint smile. 'Yes, darling. Better every day.'

I felt Ivanka's frown before I saw it. 'You're still in pain, aren't you?' she said shrewdly, entering the room. 'Agata, get your hand away. Children, the television is over there. You are to leave Babcia alone while she watches you, do you understand?'

'They're fine–' I began.

Ivanka interrupted with a wagging finger. 'They can look after themselves, mother. Which is more than I can say for you. Here.'

She retrieved the tray that she had been setting up in the kitchen. It was laden with a steaming pot of black tea, a hot plate of mushroom pierogi, and a dish of carrot salad with pickled cucumber spilling over the side. As if she thought I were in danger of wasting away, there was also a wobbling stack of apple pancakes and a generous slice of poppy-seed roll perched precariously on the edge.

Ivanka set it down on the table by my chair. 'Do you need anything else?'

I eyed the tray of provisions with resentment. 'You're only going out for half an hour,' I replied.

I knew she had only fixed it for me on the assumption that I couldn't do it myself. Ivanka rarely made such an effort in the kitchen.

'Did you bake this?' I asked, pointing to the cake.

Her eyes narrowed at me. 'It's from the store. You think I have the time to make any of this from scratch?'

'Well, I'm sure it's lovely,' I said sniffily.

I shuffled uncomfortably in my chair. A

modern, straight-backed thing with shallow cushions upholstered in sweaty PVC. I missed my own armchair.

*I would be more comfortable in my own home,* I continually told Ivanka. But my entreaties fell upon deaf ears. Ivanka took control as soon as the hospital were done with me, and thus I'd been living in her house – against my will, I should add – since my accident.

Ivanka insisted it was the only way to take care of me. I didn't recall asking to be taken care of.

I poked at the salad on my tray. 'Still no meat, I notice.'

'No. I'm still vegetarian, mother.'

'Wouldn't mind a bit of sausage every now and then,' I grumbled. 'I'd make it myself. Won't trouble you.'

Truth be told, I didn't overly mind Ivanka's cooking, but I'd take any excuse to get my hands on some fresh meat – and a way out of this house. The dragon was on my mind. It was more than a month since Smok last had a full meal. A month of unwary dog-walkers and trail hikers strolling yards from his front door. I kept a firm eye on the news for reports of missing persons. None so far.

Yet, as soon as I entertained that thought, I swung back to pitying Smok. Worrying that the dragon might, in fact, starve without me.

There was something quite helpless about the creature. The way it couldn't seem to squeeze all the way out of its cave. The way its scales occasionally dropped off like peeling flakes of dry paint. Surely it was once a fine and fearsome beast. How brittle we become in our old age.

I picked up my argument as Ivanka walked past again. 'Or I could do a good chicken soup,' I suggested. 'Easy to make. Fortifying. If you let me go to the shops for you–'

Ivanka was only half-listening, suddenly breaking up a scuffle between the triplets. 'Henryk, you give Filip his toy back *now*. Or I shall take it away from all of you! Yes, *I will!*'

The toy being squabbled over lay in pieces on the floor. It seemed a regular scene in this house, which I had previously only been invited into for special occasions.

I wasn't prepared for the disarray behind the scenes of Ivanka's life. There were no still moments in her house. Everything was in motion, all the time. Even plonked in front of the television, the triplets jumped and fidgeted and fought. Ivanka herself was constantly bustling, tapping on her phone while picking up laundry while shouting at the boys from three rooms away.

Ivanka pulled away from the triplets, tugging at her hair.

'How long is Agata staying?' I asked, seeing the aforementioned child race across the room again.

'As long as she needs,' Ivanka replied irritably. 'You might spare some consideration for her mother's condition. Oh, what now?' She glanced down at her phone, harried by some new message of urgency from her colleagues. This working from home lark didn't seem to be the solution she had expected it to be.

And then of course there was Pawel, who was in and out of his Aunt Ivanka's house as though she'd installed a revolving door. I could imagine why the loud chaos of this house would be preferable to the heavy silence in his own.

Ivanka looked as though she wanted to scream at her phone, while her children squealed in play in the background.

'What is it?' I waved to get her attention. 'You

know, you could let me babysit properly. For more than half an hour. Take yourself off somewhere else to work or relax for a day.' *Perhaps then I'd have chance to feed the dragon.*

She speared me with a disparaging stare. 'How will you run after them when they get into trouble? More likely they would need to look after *you*.'

I huffed into my teacup. 'I am not some helpless old woman.'

Ivanka closed her eyes – I could see the deep breaths as she counted them. No doubt envisaging yoga poses and peace mantras in her mind. 'Mother,' she said calmly, 'you're not as young as you once were.'

'I *know* that,' I said. 'I've lost my mobility, not my wits!'

Behind her, the triplets were tussling again. 'I'm the Wawel Dragon!' Henryk roared, before jumping on top of Emil.

Their game stirred the awful cauldron of worry in my chest. I hadn't left Smok on good terms. And all that talk of eating children . . . I fretted about what lengths it might go to, if it began to truly starve. Was I certain it couldn't leave the cave? How far could its voice carry, with the newly opened path only a hundred yards away?

'Where's Agata disappeared to?' I asked suddenly.

'Hmm?' Ivanka bobbed from her phone to the triplets and back. 'She was here a moment ago . . .'

'The garden,' I said sharply, pointing out the window. 'How did she get out there?'

Ivanka dropped her phone. 'I must have left the door open . . .' She rushed to rescue her niece, who was about to intimately inspect the ornamental pond.

I poked at my food while she was outside. Lifting the teapot dislodged a piece of paper – a leaflet. I picked it up with distaste.

*Welcome to The Pogodny Residential Care Home*, it declared in pretty pastel colours. *Enjoy the independence of assisted living in our bright, compassionate facility. Providing person-centred care, with dignity.*

I scoffed loudly and waved the leaflet as Ivanka returned with Agata gripped tightly in hand. 'What's this not-so-subtle hint for? I'm old – not incapable!'

'Just a suggestion, mother,' Ivanka replied

through gritted teeth. She ushered Agata to join the boys, two of whom had already disappeared from sight. 'I want you to think about it. I know you don't enjoy being here with us.' She added under her breath: 'Though I'm doing my best,'

'When I am better, I shall go home,' I said pointedly. 'To *my home.*'

Ivanka adjusted the cushioned stool under my leg. 'But should you? This accident might be a sign. You've been struggling on your own for a while now.'

I sucked in a shocked breath. 'I have not been *struggling.*'

'No? Is that why I found a dead mouse under your cabinets last month?' Ivanka's foot began to tap. 'Is that why the dust is inches thick on the carpets in your house? Don't get me started on the clutter. And the kitchen – good god. There was food rotting in your fridge, mother! How many roast chickens does one woman need?'

She tucked her arms against her chest as though suppressing the urge to truly explode. 'I do what I can for you. But there are only so many dishes I can wash and clothes I can fold in a day. I can't look after your house and my own.'

'I have *never* asked you to be my maid,' I said, drawing myself up in my chair. 'You make me sound pitiful!'

'Have you seen yourself?' she snapped back. 'You're in clean clothes today. When was the last time you'd changed your skirts, before coming here? I've seen you in the same blouse for weeks straight. You wear a headscarf so we won't see the state of your hair. Are you struggling to get into the bath? I know you are. I saw everything you'd knocked over from your last attempt!'

'How dare you!' I shouted. 'I've never heard anything so *disrespectful!*'

By the television, Emil shrunk away from our voices and kept glancing to the door. I saw the faces of Agata, Henryk, and Filip peering round it with worried expressions. Mindful of their ears, I dropped my voice. 'Perhaps you should look to your children before you start trying to control your mother.'

Ivanka's shoulders heaved. In a low voice she shot back, 'At least I am doing better for them than you and Dad ever did for us.'

She turned before the rebuke could lash from

my tongue. *Insolent girl,* I wanted to scream. *Do you know the sacrifices I made?*

'You have your food,' Ivanka declared to the room. 'Boys, you know where the TV remote is. Fetch Babcia more tea if she needs it, and look after Agata. I won't be long at the shops. Babcia will watch you until I'm home. *Be good.*'

She didn't look back at me before fetching her coat and striding to the door. It closed with a sullen click in her wake.

Breathlessly, the children looked between themselves for encouragement. I could read their faces. *Babcia is angry.*

I stared down at my knuckles. They shook in my lap.

I breathed deeply through my nostrils.

Unclasping my fists, I said, 'Come to Babcia, children. Everything is all right.'

They huddled round me. Agata let me pull her onto my knee for a cuddle.

'We don't think you smell,' Henryk was kind enough to confide in my ear.

'Only of pickles,' agreed Filip.

'And sometimes eggs,' said Emil.

I strangled a bitter laugh. 'Thank you.'

Maybe Ivanka was right. I thought of my cluttered house. There were corners of it I hadn't seen for years. Corners of myself I hadn't seen for years. Even my mirrors were black with grime.

So much easier, to not look yourself in the eye.

Henryk was itching to say something.

I sighed. 'Stop fidgeting, boy. What do you want to ask?'

He mumbled the question. 'What did Ma mean, about you and Dad?'

It took a moment to untangle their unique worldview. 'Not your dad, Henryk. She meant her own father. My husband.' I closed my eyes, gave a rueful huff. 'He could be a real dragon, sometimes.'

'Like the Wawel Dragon?' asked Emil.

'No, that's not–' I caught the look on his face and realised the question was not so much a serious one as it was a plea for Babcia to return to the familiar ground of legends and fairy tales.

'Well. Why not,' I murmured. 'My husband and the dragon had a lot in common. You see, a dragon's roar can shake the very ground you stand on. Their breath smells of rotten pickles – and your grandfather was always one for pickles. Their temperament is selfish, only thinking of food and themselves. All in all, dragons are very unpleasant beasts.'

'Yuk,' agreed Agata, snuggling into my chest.

The children settled around me, simultaneously soothed and excited by the tones of a story in the making.

'What does the Wawel Dragon look like, Babcia?' Henryk asked, bouncing slightly.

I considered Smok in his cave, withered and dull with his teeth falling out. 'He's an ugly fellow,' I said. 'Claws as long as kitchen knives, and twice as sharp. Because he lives in a cave, he is adapted for the dark. His eyes are pale as though blind, but don't be fooled . . . his nose more than makes up for the lack of sight. He–'

'Do you know where his cave is, Babcia?' Emil butted in. I frowned at the interruption, but before I could answer he blurted out news that made my heart clench. 'Pawel's gone to find it!'

'What do you mean by that?' I said sharply. Agata clutched at me, frightened by the change in my tone.

The boys shared another round of nervous glances. *Are we in trouble?*

Tentatively, Henryk spoke for the rest of them. 'Pawel's been out exploring in the woods, that's all. He doesn't like being home much.' He stood tugging at his t-shirt while I processed this. A thousand permutations ran through my brain.

'Which woods?' I said, a little hoarsely.

'By the park. He told us yesterday he found a new path,' Henryk said.

Emil nudged him excitedly. 'Tell her about the cave!'

'Oh, yeah! Pawel said there's a *cave*,' Henryk continued, apparently emboldened. 'Dragons in it, for sure.'

*No.*

I rose with a start, jolting Agata out of my lap. Pain lanced through my leg as it bore some weight. I grabbed for my new crutches – blasted, unwelcome things – and hobbled past the stunned children into Ivanka's kitchen.

Four pairs of eyes watched me, with no small measure of alarm, as I rattled through Ivanka's cupboards, tossing jars and cans onto the counter like trash. *Not this, not this, nor this one.* I finally chanced upon her cleaning supplies, tucked up almost too high for me to reach. I tottered on one leg as I stretched up for the bottle of bleach.

'Um,' stammered Emil, as I read the label, 'Mum said you aren't to do any housework . . .'

I grunted a non-response and moved to open the fridge. Staring at the packed shelves of fresh vegetables and soy-based proteins, I let out a deep, frustrated groan. Of course there would be no real chicken in this house. But on the counter, a large jar of pickled herrings caught my eye. It would be heavy. But the smell of vinegar might mask the scent of chemicals.

I set to unscrewing the jar and drained some of the brine into the sink. Then I topped it up with a liberal, pungent dose of undiluted bleach.

Little gasps broke through my concentrated stupor.

'Why are you doing that, Babcia?' Emil asked meekly.

'Don't worry, children,' I said. 'No one is going to eat these.'

I screwed the cap back on and shook the jar vigorously. The silvery fish became obscured by a milky cloud in the liquid. I was breathing heavily,

I noticed. Too much effort. Too much exertion, just this one little act.

'I am going out,' I announced. I pointed a crutch at the four children. 'I am going to look for Pawel, do you understand? He may be in some serious danger. You are *not* to leave this house. You are *not* to squabble, and you are *not* to tell your mother where I've gone. Are we clear?'

Wide-eyed, they offered shallow nods. 'But where *are* you going, Babcia?' Henryk pressed.

'To kill a dragon,' I replied grimly.

They followed my laborious journey to the front door. Click, thump. Click, thump. The awful awkward hopping of a cripple. I tied my headscarf ruthlessly tight under my chin and donned my heaviest overcoat. The jar of poisoned herrings was large, but my pockets were larger, so it nestled snugly within one as I turned to the children for the last time and squared my shoulders. Agata hung behind the triplets with her curls falling across her face. They all shared the same expression, a cocktail of bewilderment and fear.

*Ivanka will be home soon,* I told myself. *They are safe here.*

'Be good,' I said.

And locked the door behind me.

\* \* \*

It shouldn't have taken an hour to reach Smok's cave, but my graceless hopping gait demanded it. Instead of my usual route I took the newly opened footpath. I nodded stiffly to concerned joggers and dog-walkers who passed me by. *Should she be out here alone?* their eyes said, staring at my booted foot.

The thing was like a manacle, dragging me down. But I dragged it, all the same.

I found my decaying patch of warning signs and hobbled off the path. *Warning. eep Out.* I brushed a hand over the sign to dislodge some material that was caught in the branches, obscuring the *K*. It came away easily, a long scarf of striped wool. I stared at the pattern. Yellow and green stripes. Pawel's scarf.

'*Pawel!* His name ripped from my throat like the panicked cry of a wounded deer. I spun as fast as my crutches would allow in a tottering circle. The dark trees closed in around me. Pawel was nowhere to be seen.

Ignoring the throb in my broken leg, I slithered down the slope to Smok's cave. I landed on my rear with another slice of pain arcing through my hip, but still propelled myself forward again. My crutches slipped every other step in the carpet of leaves and mud.

I bent low to Smok's cave and bawled into it. 'Smok! Come out, you vile beast!'

My only reply was a thin echo bouncing back to me. In it, I heard the terror in my voice.

Fighting the tremors in my hands, I patted the jar of poisoned herring in my pocket. 'Do you hear me?' I shouted again. 'I've brought food. You must be hungry, old boy.'

The last was a hope, an invocation, a desperate plea. Please be hungry. Please do not be full of child meat.

A sob wracked from my throat. Still there was no answer.

The cave receded a long way into darkness. Nothing but bleak shadows met my scrutiny.

Perhaps the dragon had starved. Or perhaps it lived, but was too weak to have caught a child with as much energy and strength as Pawel. Surely the boy had more sense than to be drawn wilfully into the jaws of a monster.

*Come to my cave little ones, don't be scared. Come play in these depths little children, let me show you my lair. Such wonders, such treasures ...*

The dragon's words coiled around my heart. I stared into the cave's menacing depths.

I would have to crawl.

Slowly, I sank to my hands and knees. The crutches dropped in place. They'd be no use underground.

My kneecap met the ground gently, through a cushion of skirts, and I let out a low moan.

Until now, my broken leg had enjoyed a certain numbness, a detachment, while I kept weight-bearing duties away from it. Now it tingled; anxious pricking pins as my muscles woke up. A low-burning fire in the middle of my tibia which threatened to turn molten with too much pressure.

I stretched out my hands and crawled forward. My progress could be measured in mere inches per minute. Soil pattered onto my back as I awkwardly scraped my way under the overhanging rock. Soon I was beneath a ceiling of stone. The light dimmed as my own body blocked its course from the entrance.

My path was a black hole ahead. Under my calloused fingers the rock was slick with water and patches of thinning moss. The ground was surprisingly level, almost smooth. I recalled the sound of the dragon emerging from the depths, grinding stone against its belly. As darkness closed in deeper, the shadows blended into one another and I could no longer make out the shape of the passage.

Breathing noisily, I half-crawled, half-shunted forward on my stomach, at times letting my injured leg drag uselessly while the rest of my body did the work. Pricking pins turned to stabbing needles. An undercurrent of nausea now rose and fell with every movement.

At one point I lifted my head too high – my headscarf snagged on a jutting rock. It pulled taut about my throat. I choked. Panic flared. I scrabbled at my neck to release the knot. The scarf fell away behind me, lost to the dark.

I felt the darkness take me, too. It crawled into my ears, up my nostrils. Stuffed itself into my mouth as I breathed the warm, fetid air. It slid down my throat and into my stomach – into all the darkest parts of me. It had been there all along.

*I must stop,* I thought in a haze. *I will die down here.*

The darkness coiled in my mind.

*So will Pawel, if I don't find him.*

Sudden movement startled me. Some shape, up close, indistinct. And yet the darkness was so complete, so whole, I couldn't fathom it. I blinked rapidly, and the movement revealed itself to be the coloured flashes you perceive behind your eyelids when you squeeze them closed. They hovered in the air in front of my face. A flashing hallucination of red dots and stripes overlaying the awful, everlasting night.

I closed my eyes, but the effect was exactly the

same. As I continued crawling, I began to forget whether my eyes were open or closed. I lost all sense of time and place. There was only the cold stone rasping against my skin, and all the intensifying pains that strung my body together. The groaning of cartilage against bone in my wrists. The dull ache within both depleted hips. A spine that has spent too many winters motionless in an armchair. Rotting teeth in over-sugared gums. Stiff shoulders, stiff knees, stiff toes – a body getting ready to become stiff all over.

I fell forward into open space. A short drop beneath my hands, leaving the rest of me scrabbling for purchase on the unseen rocks. With it came a faint sense of echo. The tunnel I was in had widened, become a chamber of sorts. I slithered into it, dragging my leg like a piece of useless fat.

'Pawel?' I tremored. More phantasms swam in front of my eyes, pretending to be the shape of a boy. There was no answer.

I inched forward, perceiving different geology in this space. The rock floor was coarser, and was littered with loose stones that knocked away from my hands. I grabbed one and found it strangely long and smooth, and much lighter than I thought a stone should be.

'*Mother?*'

The voice startled me. It was so faint, I was sure it existed only in my mind. I twisted around – stupid, I realised at once, because it lost my bearings. Was I facing forward now, or back the way I had come? New panic set into my chest. How could I save anyone if I was lost in this cave?

My breath squeezed into a pathetic word. 'Help.'

'Mother?' One of the flashing phantasms morphed, became a speck of true light in the distance, white and absurd in this place. Was that Ivanka's voice?

Her face, a pale ghost, seemingly disembodied, floated out of the nothing. The shining light spilled over me, forced me to squint in visual pain. For the first time I glimpsed the grime on my clothes, the holes where fabric had torn on jagged edges. Ivanka gasped – the sound seemed to fill the entire cave.

She scrambled towards me on all fours through the low passage, finally toppling into the larger chamber with me. She shone the light – the torch from her phone – into my face. '*Mother!* What are doing in here? Have you gone *mad?*'

I could tell she meant it. There was a fear in her voice beyond the natural dread of the dark and tight spaces.

'How did you find me?' The words rattled out of my mouth more harshly than I'd intended. 'It's dangerous in here!'

'I agree,' Ivanka hissed. 'That's why I'm going to take to you home.' She waved something, a scrap of fabric, difficult to make out in the shadows behind the phone. My headscarf, I realised.

'*How dare you* leave the children alone!' Ivanka said. 'Of course they told me where you went. And your crutches are outside. What were you *thinking?*'

'I'm looking for Pawel–'

'You are *very ill.*' Her hand grasped mine. For the first time I noticed I was trembling.

'Pawel isn't in here, mother,' Ivanka said. 'Listen to me. *Listen.* I ran into him on my way here. He was coming to find me, in fact! *He* found this cave. *He* saw your crutches outside it. *He* was sensible enough to not go in!'

All at once my soul lifted, buoyed on a current of relief. Ivanka squeezed my hand, watching me carefully.

My voice dwindled to a squeak. 'Pawel is safe?'

'I sent him home.'

Her hand pulled back and I knew it was because I was suddenly shaking. I cried with stilted sobs that bounced back off the cold stone. 'It would have been my fault. If he'd died it would have been my fault.' I looked into her eyes. 'I've always wanted to do better for you. For them.'

'Mother . . .'

Ivanka shifted up next to me, hugging my shoulders. Her light swung down, illuminating the cave floor. Our eyes naturally followed it.

Ivanka's breath hitched. We both went very still.

Bones. The ground was littered with piles of loose bones.

'Animals,' Ivanka said breathlessly. Her fingers curled into mine. 'Must be animals that got trapped down here.'

Her hand wobbled as she pointed the light into all corners of the cave. It was a large cavern, stretching into unknown distance. The bones also stretched into the darkness. Some of them shone brightly, picked clean to a glossy yellow-white. Others were caked in dirt, stained with a dark pigment that extended up the cave walls–

I pulled my eyes away quickly. We were in the heart of the dragon's den.

'Bears,' Ivanka said. She stood up, spinning in a slow, nervous circle. 'It could be bears live here.'

*Who knows how far away the dragon is,* I thought. It could be watching us at that very moment. 'We need to move,' I said.

Ivanka's light fell on something that gleamed amid the bones. She hesitated, then stooped to pick it up. It was a brass pocket watch. She stared at it, nestled snugly in the palm of her hand.

'Let's go,' I said, a little too sharply. I turned on my stomach and began to crawl back to the tunnel.

'Wait! Let me help you,' Ivanka hissed frantically. 'You're not going to get far like that!'

I shrugged her off. 'I got this far,' I muttered, gritting teeth behind my walls of creaking pain. 'Leave me be.'

Ivanka clattered behind me, displacing bones as she moved. Although she kept her voice low, it was shaped like a barb. 'For once in your life, *accept my help.*'

Her hands dug under my armpits. I yowled in pain as she lifted me, pulled me upright into a sitting position. My leg snagged on something and I gave an involuntary blubber.

'I'm sorry.' Her hands cupped my face. 'But you need to stop putting weight on that. Do you think I'm blind? I can *see* you're in pain. Let me pull you out on your back. We'll go slow.'

Her hands stopped fussing, and I registered the sound that must have caught her attention. A distant slithering in the dark. The crunching and cracking of bone.

I snatched at Ivanka's arm. 'Get out of here. Leave. Go! *Go!*'

'I'm not leaving you.'

She cast her light in a quick motion behind us, scoping the way out, before tucking it away in a pocket. Then she grabbed me under the arms again and hoisted me along the ground. Her breath was wet and hot on my neck. I bit down on my tongue to keep from screaming. My leg bounced from rock to rock like a piece of dead meat.

*'Who enters my lair?'*

The dragon's voice rumbled out of the dark. Ivanka gasped into my hair and we both fell still.

*'I hear you. I smell you. Old woman. Have you finally come to feed me?'*

Smok drew nearer. I heard its massive bulk dragging over the floor of bones.

*'Did you forget me? Did you spurn me? Where is your pity now, old woman?'*

I cleared my throat. My voice wobbled. 'I have come to feed you, old Smok. Worried about you, I was. I've been laid up, you see and–'

*'You abandoned me. Discarded me.'*

Ivanka curled up against my back. She squirmed, reaching for her phone.

'Don't–' I tried to say.

But she'd already pulled it out. The beam of white light strobed through the cave, hitting the dragon square in its milky eyes.

Smok roared. It was a guttural, spluttering sound, made no less terrifying by the missing teeth in its gums. Ivanka stifled a scream.

She scrabbled to try to pull me back some

more, but I wrestled away and dug into my pocket for the jar of pickled, poisoned herring.

Smok hauled itself toward me. I waved the glass jar in the air frantically. 'Food!' I shouted hoarsely. 'I brought you tasty food!'

Smok was on top of me. Its snout dragged over my skirt and pushed into my stomach. With one shake of its head, the jar was knocked clean out of my hand. The gaping nostrils levelled with my face. Smok blew out a stream of foul, clammy air.

*'Your meagre offerings can sate me no longer.'* Globs of saliva dripped onto my blouse. *'Today, I shall feast!'*

The jaws opened wide. Wide enough to swallow my head. I closed my eyes, ready to meet my husband on the other side.

A fleshy *thump* closed the jaws before they reached me – Ivanka brought both fists down onto the dragon's snout. Her phone dropped to the ground, spilling its light upwards and illuminating long stalactites hanging from the cave roof like teeth.

The dragon recoiled, now an obscured shape

in the darkness. It grunted, swaying from side to side. Sniffing.

'Run!' I yelled to Ivanka.

Smok's head veered in her direction.

I lunged between them – a briefly standing pillar of agony, and then a sobbing lump as my leg collapsed beneath me. The dragon's jaws plunged down. Gums and broken teeth clamped over my plastic-booted foot. Like a crocodile, the jaws locked tight. Horrid pressure fixed around my leg.

The plastic cracked. I screamed.

Ivanka's ragged breathing swam in and out of my ears. I'd lost any ability to discern where she was. My entire world was consumed by broiling pain. Smok's jaws closed tighter, began to tug. I was a whimpering ball. Very dimly, I became aware of a frantic thumping that might have been Ivanka punching the dragon's nose over and over again.

I deserved this. Me, the fool who would let a dragon live near my children. I should have dispatched of it; another danger I should have seen and done away with sooner. But guilt kept me from killing old Smok. Not pity, or kindness. Just guilt.

I lost consciousness for a few seconds, and awoke to new torments. Having thought I'd reached my limit, the very peak of what pain I could comprehend, a fresh fire now ignited in my left hip. Smok was trying to pull my leg from its socket. I dragged on the ground with each tug, burbling mad nothings into the dark.

'Let him eat me,' I tried to tell Ivanka. 'Get out of here. Save yourself.'

A shriek pierced through the cave. Ivanka, screaming, but not in pain. The dragon jerked its head, pulling me like a ragdoll. In a motley of shadows I glimpsed Ivanka latched onto its skull, her mouth open against its scales. Screaming into its ears.

Smok thrashed, trying to throw her off. My head smacked against rock. The leg – for it was no longer *my* leg, existing in its own realm, dislocated, certainly – bent at unnatural angles as I was yanked to and fro. A final *crack* and the boot slid off my foot in pieces.

The dragon flinched backwards, jaws snapping closed. Now free of me, it shook Ivanka off with ease. She landed next to me amid the bones.

Smok reared. It huffed and snorted, then gave a

guttural, strangled growl. The muscles in its throat convulsed. The dragon smacked its head onto the ground, gagging like it was trying to throw up. My boot was stuck in its throat.

'Said you should chew, didn't I?' I croaked.

'*W-witch,*' the dragon gargled.

The pale head smacked onto the ground again and again, trying to dislodge the obstruction. Ivanka stumbled to my side, grasping her phone. She dragged me out of range of the dragon's thrashing. It broke stalactites from the ceiling as it reared onto its hind legs – I glimpsed a long, serpentine body, and the stubs of decrepit wings. Rock smashed down around us.

Smok fell on its back. The talons on its stubby legs raked uselessly at the air. Its massive bulk quivered, entering death throes. Suddenly it was only an animal; its dying snorts were pathetic and helpless. I reached out a hand, as if to comfort it, though there was no way I could move myself closer. Smok's last sounds were the muted glugging of its throat muscles as it lay down to die.

Finally, the dragon was still.

The last crumbs of rock pattered onto the ground, and the bones settled from their rattling.

Ivanka pointed her phone at the dragon's face. The milky eyes still stared into the cave's distance. A sheen on the scales might have been sweat, or simply moisture from its underground home. Ivanka watched it for a while. There was no more movement, no twitch, no breath. The dragon was dead.

My whimpering drew her attention back to me. She dropped to her knees and ran shocked hands over my hips, my leg. The exposed plaster cast was shredded, and something oozed from within. I cringed away, wailed as she touched my flesh.

'I'm sorry, I'm sorry,' she gasped. Then buried her head in my neck and cried.

'You're a strong girl,' I mumbled. I glanced at the dragon and a twisted laugh escaped my throat. 'The stories are true. Cobbler got you in the end, old Smok.'

I waved at my mangled foot in answer to Ivanka's exhausted, questioning gaze. She didn't seem to see the funny side.

'Let's get you to a hospital,' she said.

Our escape from the cave took at least an hour. I was truly immobilised, empty of everything but joy that my daughter and grandchildren were all safe and alive. Ivanka strapped my legs together using my headscarf. Then, with gruelling determination, she lugged me backwards down the tight passageway, through the dark, until cool forest air graced our lips again.

We waited some distance away from the cave for a paramedic team to arrive. While she cradled my head, Ivanka turned the brass pocket watch over in her hands.

'How long have you known about the dragon, mother?' she said quietly.

I pretended to doze, but it didn't fool her.

'I know you hear me,' she said.

I opened one eye and mumbled, 'I've always tried to protect you.'

'You told us he walked out on you.'

'I wish it had been so easy.' I exhaled deeply. 'No. He made it clear he was never leaving, and that there was *nothing* I could do. And I believed that. Until one day, at my lowest ebb, I walked a path less travelled in the woods . . . and discovered an unexpectedly occupied cave . . .'

I trailed off, staring into the memory. How easy it had been, to lure him down here. The lie of a hidden cache of whisky was all it had taken.

He was so willing to take what wasn't his. And I'd watched, dutifully, as per his demands, hiding purple bruises under a pretty pinafore dress, while he stuck his head into that dark hole. The first of many meals.

As though offerings of chicken and sausages could atone for a capital sin. Perhaps keeping one monster alive, in place of another.

Ivanka whispered in my ear, a secret and a truth. 'When I was little, I wondered why you never hit him back. I thought you were weak. I understood later that you were a wall. A shield in front of me and Jozef. But I was still angry with you.' She nuzzled into my neck. 'So angry that you never asked anyone for help.'

'Oh, but I did.' I grunted a chuckle. 'I asked a dragon.'

Ivanka snapped the pocket watch closed. She hugged me tighter, and we waited in soft silence until the ambulance crew arrived.

\* \* \*

T hree months later, I woke from a comfortable slumber in my own armchair, in Ivanka's living room. The triplets were in their usual spot, playing with dinosaurs on the floor in front of the television. Agata drew with crayons in a colouring book on the couch. Pawel sat in the corner with his back against the wall, mouth screwed into a frown while he contemplated his maths homework.

Ivanka brought in a tray of juice and biscuits. The children dropped their activities and crowded round for snacks. She shared a brief smile in my direction.

'The removal men have just finished,' she told me. 'Give me a few hours to unpack, and your room will be ready for you.'

'Thank you,' I said, sincerely.

'Can you watch the children for me? I'll get some sausages for your dinner.'

I shrugged indifference, a movement that nevertheless made me wince with residual aches. 'Don't trouble yourself. I'd rather eat with my family. What are you doing tonight?'

'A vegetable goulash.'

'With potato pancakes?' I said hopefully.

She smiled. 'If you'll show me how to make them.'

She left to finish organising the amalgamation of my possessions into her family home. The sale of my old house would finalise in a few weeks, and Ivanka didn't know yet that I'd be giving a generous portion to her and her husband. The rest I'd arranged to be set aside for the children.

I carefully shifted my bad leg on its stool. A framework of steel pins now held it together. I would be on a crutch for the rest of my life. But that didn't matter, so long as I could spend it with the people I loved.

Henryk nudged his brothers. They'd noticed I was awake. Five pairs of eyes settled on their battered grandmother. A woman who they were used to hearing stories from, but who lately had been the topic of all sorts of stories while she rested in the hospital. They were clever kids. And Pawel, despite all the warnings Ivanka had thrown at him, had almost certainly returned to explore the cave where his aunt had pulled his grandmother out of the jaws of death.

As a group, they assembled on the floor in front of me. Hushed with reverence, eyes wide as saucers. Agata broke the silence, and I got the feel she'd been nominated by her cousins. In a whisper that made my heart swell, she said:

'Tell us about the dragon, Babcia.'

## *About the Author*

Georgina Jeffery is a British author of speculative fiction. Her stories often blend elements of fantasy, humour, and horror, and tend to reflect her fascination with folklore from around the world. You'll find mythical beasties, malevolent spirits, and eldritch magic in a lot of her writing.

Georgina's work can be found in a variety of anthologies and journals, including *The NoSleep Podcast, Unbreakable Ink, The San Cicaro Experience,* and *Copperfield Review Quarterly.*

# ALSO BY GEORGINA JEFFERY

### The Jack Hansard Series: Season One

Funny urban fantasy with a lot of British folklore. Jack Hansard, occult salesman, turns reluctant detective when his merchandise is stolen and becomes embroiled in a supernatural kidnapping case.

### The Jack Hansard Series: Season Two

Jack Hansard and his coblyn friend Ang are back in business. Together they face shapeshifters, piskies, and ancient magics in their quest to track down Ang's missing kin and uncover the secrets of Baines & Grayle.

### Beyond Thundering Waters (Dark Folklore)

A dark fairy tale in a modern Norwegian setting. When a young girl meets a huldra in the Norwegian wilderness, she unwittingly makes a supernatural bargain that puts her Pappa's life at stake.

### Across Screaming Seas (Dark Folklore)

A dark fairy tale in a modern Welsh setting. A diver finds herself trapped in a mermaid's lair, wrestling against her own conscience and the need to survive.

## The Hub

A supernatural short story with a sci-fi edge. When an app developer accidentally creates a maliciously benevolent social media network, only her girlfriend can save her from what she's brought to life

Lightning Source UK Ltd.
Milton Keynes UK
UKHW011258181122
412419UK00005B/78